T0129002

Ascension of Satan

A Fact-Finding Mission to Question God about His Failed
Promises and Sole Pretensions to Creation.

JEMADARI VI-BEE-KIL KILELE

Ascension of Satan. Frontispiece by Prince Mundeke, 2011

Order this book online at www.trafford.com
or email orders@trafford.com

Most Trafford titles are also available at major online book retailers.

Printed in the United States of America.

ISBN: 978-1-4669-0250-3 (sc)
ISBN: 978-1-4669-0206-0 (e)

Library of Congress Control Number: 2011919604

Trafford rev. 07/20/2012

 www.trafford.com

North America & international
toll-free: 1 888 232 4444 (USA & Canada)
phone: 250 383 6864 ♦ fax: 812 355 4082

CONTENTS

LIST OF CHARACTERS

1. God
2. The Chief Protocol
3. Ndoki Machine
4. Satan
5. God's cabinet members
6. Sperm Matozoid
7. Voltaire
8. Kraft Buganga
9. Mrs. Nda Kulya
10. Kasebo Lwenzo.
11. Karl Marx
12. Joseph Stalin
13. Jean-Paul Sartre
14. Lunyego Kitwanda
15. René Descartes

FOREWORD

Religious fanaticism distances people from the lane of knowledge and self-control. It leads them astray until they are kept totally ignorant.

However, the truth is always there, within us. On the one side, it takes one person to dare unearth it and bring it to the fore. While on the other, it calls for willing persons to approach it and make it theirs. For, to be heard or discovered, the truth does not herald in churches, synagogues, mosques, or on the streets. It keeps quiet until its magnitude crashes lie. Lie is a professional talker, because it fears to be exposed . . .

By daring to read this book, you are undertaking an odyssey of freeing yourself from the prison mind-boggling of religions you've been *celled* in. To many victims of the pandemic of religions and cults, they will find it shocking to bring their "God" together with Satan. Awful, satanic, blasphemy—isn't it? But any sober person will realise that it's possible, because both guys always meet.

If "God" did not want to meet Satan, right from "creating" him, and after Satan allegedly disobeyed him, he would already have passed a supreme sentence on him: capital punishment. Rather, he let him go, and the latter continues to reign supreme on Earth despite the many speculations of lie-drunken and sick preachers that torment the world.

In this second book (after **The Trial of Satan**), I am still battling to liberate the million captives who have been threatened by blind faith due to fear of death, destruction, wrath, fire burning and other forms of punishment from the *Almighty* biblical "God" of Israel, who has been adored ever since we have existed.

The refusal to read this book is the acceptance of slavery and a life of perpetual fear. It is about time to fathom new mines of knowledge and liberate oneself from a slavery and sheepish mentality that has abusively been seeded in us by money-mongers who claim to be exclusively talking to their "God." God? Hey!

As Michael Tellinger puts it: *"Our arrogance is our weakness and our ignorance, a congenital disease that will eventually destroy us."*

J. Kilele

ASCENSION OF SATAN

ACT 1: SCENE I

(*His Excellency Mr. Satan, president of the Democratic Republic of Earth [DRE] is being diplomatically received by the Most High God, President of the Theocratic Republic of Heavens [TRH]. Mr. Satan is accompanied by his delegation team composed of Voltaire, Karl Marx, René Descartes, Joseph Stalin, and Jean-Paul Sartre. The ceremony takes place at Skulls & Bones chambers, the presidential palace. God is seated in the middle of the hall, dressed in his fabulous royal attire. Other members of the theocratic government are attending the welcoming ceremony. The Chief Protocol hands over a file to His Majesty God, who opens and reads it. Then . . .)*

God.

And who is the next guest this morning?

(*Enter the Chief Protocol.*)

Chief Protocol (*Holding an audience log book*).

Your Majesty, the next visitor after the ambassador of the Republic of Sin Purgatory (RSP) is His Excellence Mr. Satan, the Devil.

Jemadari Vi-Bee-Kil Kilele

God.

Let him in. It has been quite a while since I have heard of that guy. Let him in, please.

Chief Protocol.

Right away, Your Highness. (*Exit.*)

God (*Talking to the standing members of the government.*)

I can't doubt the chap is leading a powerful delegation to here. I pray you, Mr. Ndoki Machine, you who is a specialist in celestial legal matters and custodian of all files related to my relationship with this guy, to be attentive to what he is going to say.

Ndoki Machine.

Unfailingly, I will, Your Majesty.

God (*Talking to Ndoki Machine again, his specialist attorney.*)

The guy is too vocal on any issues pertaining to our partnership and power sharing in the secret of the making of the world. So, while he will be ranting, ensure that you identify his contradictions so that later on we nail him down.

Chief Protocol (*Returning ahead of the visiting delegation. The members of the divine government are seated all around God.*)

All rise. Ladies and Gentlemen, His Excellency Mr. Satan, the Devil, Lucifer, President of the Democratic Republic of Earth, on a special and courtesy visit to our TCR—otherwise

Theocratic Celestial Republic. Oh! I beg your pardon. I meant to say—our TRH, Theocratic Republic of Heaven. Again, all rise and bow in his honour and for his full respect. (*Satan advances toward God's central seat, followed by two aides while three members of his delegation remain standing at the outskirts of the hall.*)

God (R*ising up and stretching his arms.*)

In my arms, comrade Lucifer.

Satan

It has been a long while since we last met.

God

Tell you what, comrade. I keep on thinking about that day we parted. It was really not on a good note at all, but . . .

Satan

Yes, indeed, comrade. Here I am, finally; and not alone, comrade. Allow me to introduce to you my colleagues.

God

Oh! What a pleasure.

Satan

Starting on my right hand side; this is Jean-Paul Sartre, Minister of the Existentialism and in charge of questioning all matters pertaining to your existence. Next is Mr. Karl Marx, Minister of International Labour and sworn enemy of capitalism and globalisation. This is René Descartes, an exceptional scholar at the Ministry of All Methodical Doubts. And finally, here is Mr. Voltaire, a sworn atheist. Minister of Rationality and staunch human rights defender. Retain that, he also is an erstwhile writer who suffered persecution by the French King . . .

God

And this gentleman? What about him?

Satan

Sorry, I was about to forget. This is Mr. Joseph Stalin, Minister of Communism-Socialism and grand butcher of the so-called Christians and members of all other religions on Earth.

God

Waoh! Such a panel of inquisitors! Comrade, you are well surrounded. Let me tell you.

Satan

Indeed, comrade. I am happy to be here again. (*Looking up and down, then all around.*) Not much has greatly changed though. Everything looks so serene. Why?

God (*Leading him around to introduce him to his closest cabinet members.*)

Our planet remains tranquil in all its fields and core. We keep on inventing new items, of which remnants only are revealed to your planet's dwellers that call themselves scientists and inventors. Here, we don't suffer any cataclysms, because we are above the nature. In fact, we are the ones who orchestrate all cataclysms that befall your planet.

Satan

But, if I may ask, why do you do that to a world that you claim to love and protect, and whose inhabitants you have constrained to worshiping you under constant fear as a barter condition for their illusionary happiness?

God (*Turning towards Satan and touching him on the shoulder.*)

Look, comrade, cataclysms that strike your nature are a wakeup call to principles of hierarchical respect any time you disobey us. I mean me. Tsunami, volcanic eruptions, floods, earthquakes, cyclones, wars between tribes and nations, etc. are whipping measures to discipline a recalcitrant world.

Satan

Am I among the defiant elements?

God

Undoubtedly, yes . . . and this without an iota of exaggeration.

(*Satan jiggles a bit and looks at him.*).

There are still many elements under your government who fail to comply with the divine spiritual prescripts of total obedience to your creator, who I am.

Satan

I thought that glitch between you and I was over long ago, grand comrade. It's amazing how begrudging you are, after you allegedly had sent your so-called son, Jesus Christ, to redeem my people from sins they never committed and which keep on mutating from one generation to another!

God

Can you repeat what you've just said, comrade?

Satan

Pardon me?

God

You've said my so-called what?

Satan

Well, your so-called son that my people named "*Jesus Christ,*" and whom they ceaselessly keep on worshipping. [*God looks at him unhappily*] Excuse me. Did I say anything wrong?

God

Ah! (*Smiling.*)

Satan

Hey! Because, frankly speaking, you never gave a real name to this child, and he has no birth certificate. Yet you claim to be the father. It's my people who have christened him.

God

Wait a bit, wait.

Satan

No, comrade. Something is not right here. My people have been living in total confusion regarding the true identity of this guy you call your "son." Before birth, he is announced to be called Emmanuel, and once he is born, he is known as Jesus Christ, Prince of Peace, King of Kings, little Lamb, death conqueror, etc . . . . Amazingly, he has never reigned over any kingdom that we may know of. Instead, his pretentious career was short-lived by his killing. He was just a *usurper* of power. You see?

God (A*fter staring at him.*)

We'll talk about that later. (S*topping him awhile and turning his head towards the cabinet members.)* Ah, ah! I beg your pardon, Ladies and Gentlemen, for delaying to introduce to you, His *Excellency Satan,* the Devil, alias Lucifer, in our walls forever.

Satan (*Interrupting him*)

Pardon me. "Forever," you said, hey?

God

Yes. But, on our planet, there is no day, no change of atmosphere. I would say "today." But because we don't undergo modification, because we don't shape-shift, because there are no seasons nor are there any desires, wants, or needs, because there is no time line or calendar; consequently we live *forever* and *ever.* Reason why I said,

"*Welcome here forever.*" I don't mean to say, you'll be with us forever. But, as I said, that's that. Understand?

Satan

I do. And who are these guys? (*Pointing at the cabinet members.*)

God

This is His Excellency Mr. Ndoki Machine, Minister of Justice and custodian of all justice stamps, Mr. Sperm Matozoid, Minister of Fertility and Procreation; Ms. Kraft Buganga, Minister of Witchcraft, Science, and Technology; Mrs. Nda Kulya, Minister of Food Supplies, Hydrography, and Energies; Mr. Kasebo Lwenzo, Minister of Sports, Culture, and Entertainment; and finally, Mr. Lunyego Kitwanda, Minister of Defence, Wars, and Hardwares. He is the custodian of the divine arsenal—and the hardwares of warfare.

(*They then proceed inside the hall, talking, oblivious of their members' presence.*)

Satan

It's an delegation of honourable spirits whose appointment merit remains unquestionable. With such a think tank team, I tell you, you feel secure, and so is your planet.

God

Well, such is only a precaution to pre-empt any planetarian invasion, because we are not alone here. I discovered that there are other neighbour planets that were unknown to us.

Satan

How come? But, you know, even Earth geographers do not have your planet among the planetarian system. Hm! Heaven or Paradise does not really feature among human known planets. How did you come to discover others?

God

Since you left, we have been intercepting sound waves, testifying to be coming from outer space by invisible visitors who might pose a lethal menace to us.

Satan

I have been living on Earth, as you assigned me to rule over there after our dispute. However, I note that climate remained contentious between you and me ever since we clashed.

God

Wait a bit (*Holding Satan's hand, then shows him to sit down facing him. Cabinet members and Satan's delegates, who were following behind, slightly retreat backward*). I fail to understand what you mean by that, comrade.

Satan

You always entertain fictitious things from afar, comrade. I thought you were ruling in heavens and me on Earth—freely.

God

But you have the power! What else do you want from me? Where will you get a planet so populated by sheepish creatures like Earth and whose ruler remains an undisputed monarch? And that is what you are.

Satan

That's fine, comrade. But there is much to that. To many innocent and ignorant minds, the origin of sin and the reason for its existence is me. This is because of the religious intoxication from your army of liars glorified as priests, pastors, prophets, seers and you name them.

God

But they are doing their work! What is your problem?

Satan

But how can they continue to point their fingers at me, yet when you and I fought in heavens there was no witness! Who the hell tells them that I am the Prince of Evil?

God

Wait a bit. Please don't take it on that note, comrade.

Satan

Ah no. Do you gossip behind me, comrade?

God

Not really, but as we made them like us, truly speaking, they are privy to all those classified archives.

Satan (*After a pause.*)

Aaaaaah! Hence, everywhere I pass, I am the talk of the day. I am the cause of human fall and human sufferings. I am the king of all sins, and I intrude in everyone's life. Is it how the story goes?

God

I don't know exactly. But, really, who says all that? Where do you garner all those rumours?

Satan

Your worshippers point their fingers at me, accusing me of misleading them. You see?

God

They should not be doing that. I sincerely regret their deeds.

Satan

What do you say about that? Really, it's not fair. We did not agree like that, comrade.

God

Compose yourself, com . . . I created man free. You, too, are free. But your freedom is higher than theirs. Reason why you rule over them. But . . .

Satan

Ah, no. I disagree with that. The entire world is in desolation; and they question how all this can exist under your sovereignty. You claim to be infinite in wisdom and power and in love too. They tell me you are almighty and purveyor of everything.

God

I never said that. It's them who have been posting that in their literature of flattery in a bid to expect favours from me whenever they fail to get solution to their own problems. Humans never stop imploring and flattering me, even though I fail to provide for their expectations. They always would flood me with unnecessary demands, praises, and hypocritical worships. It's just funny. And they never stop, comrade . . . you see. It sometimes embarrasses me.

Satan

But to some extent, you seem to be pleased by all those forms of worship.

God

What can I do? You see; human beings often behave like a sinking ship or an aircraft in turbulence. They always send signals of pity, pity pity; signals of desperation, of rescue; a sort of 'M*ay day, May dayish*" behaviour in order to maintain the standard of their lives.

Satan

So, according to you, these people should continue to remain in such uncertainty and doubt, afflicted by woes and misery, yet in exchange to their endless prayers you promised them total happiness should they worship you?

God

But I never asked anyone not to work! You remember; we created man in our image. Consequently, if you and I are intelligent and industrious, what of people we moulded in our image? They should rely on their own. Not on me.

Satan

That's a crucial question. Even myself, I have been wondering why that man we created became too lazy; a crying baby, yet we loaded him with skills and you name it.

God

Exactly. Consequently, for the gift that we loaded them with, they must worship us; hey, my man.

Satan.

And they do pray ceaselessly. It's a sort of obsession you know. However, the material life and the happiness they long for has never come out of churches, mosques, monasteries and all those centres of manipulation.

God

Don't exaggerate, my dear. Only the cunning of them all will survive. The credulous ones will never grow mentally. I created all of you with perfect faculties to solve your daily problems. How would you expect me to solve your problems while I also have mine?

Satan (*Pauses a bit, and then looks at God.*)

13

A small portion of humanity has done their utmost to solve their problems, but another big one has failed dismally, and this is actuated by a disposition to doubt and to cavil about your capacity to rescue them.

God

You can't be the advocate of their failure. If they fail, let them fail. Is it the reason you are here?

Satan

Yes and no.

God

Be clear, comrade. You mean? Don't be dichotomous. I hate hypocrites, you know. Remember that was one of the reasons we split.

Satan

I never was a hypocrite. And I am not one up to now. You know it well. You know me. I am a straight-forward guy who never minces his words when he speaks of serious things with dictators like you. (*God gets pricked a bit and, then changes humour.*)

God

Watch your mouth.

Sata

Ah, no. You start twisting my words now. Can't you notice?

God

Watch your mouth, I say.

Satan

And my hard talking has never broken our friendship ever since. We're always together; given the delusion of your people who think that we live apart.

God *(smiling)*

Listen here, comrade. Before the entrance of evil into the world, there was peace and joy throughout the universe. All was in perfect harmony with me. All of you, my creatures, worshipped me. I gave you intelligence, freedom, wisdom, and power to watch over all the minor angels. Especially you. You were my beloved son. (*Expressing emotion.*)

Satan

I know. I know that you once loved me. That I know of. But, unlike Jesus Christ, I never knew my mother; yet you proclaim yourself my father!

God

That's trivial at this stage. Learn that I duplicate myself into both genders. Sometime I am female and some other times I am male; and the latter is the only gender you are used to.

Satan

Really?

God

I covered you with abundance and paternal love, but you personally, you, Satan, I elevated you to the highest rank. But you chose to pervert that freedom, indulging in a desire for self-exaltation, behaving yourself as my *alter ego*, and inciting the rest of the angels to move against me. And you know well that I dislike challenge. That is what provoked your fall.

Satan

But you assigned me to oversee them and to play a leadership role for them!

God

But under your tutelage, your influence over them was already rivalling, if not surpassing my own.

Satan

So you gave up?

God

To some extent, yes, I did. I didn't find it worthy to wrangle with you in a bottomless pit of unending disputes.

Satan

There you go again. Please, dry your tears. You're no different from the men I rule over on Earth. You have elevated lies and gossips to a level of art. How dare you continue with these allegations and awful calumnies that

I am the one who recruited the rest of the angels to rebel against you and to try to be more intelligent than you?

God

There is no doubt about that. You're just a cunning person. Only those who do not know you can believe in you. But . . .

Satan

You forget that we are as rational as you are, and we are able to distinguish the good from the evil. Such a faculty of reasoning helped us to decipher your treachery, and we used our freedom to go solo in our daily businesses. Do you call that rebellion? When captives liberate themselves from your bondage, you call that uprising? Mutiny? Disobedience?

God

Look, I established an order in heaven, and in departing from it, you and your blind followers dishonoured me and brought ruin upon yourselves. You have nothing to claim as compensation from me, for I owe nothing to anyone of you. I am the prime sovereign.

Satan (*After a gaze.*)

I did not come here to ask for a compensation. I came to seek a second agreement between you and me. And, if these talks fail, one of us will disappear, and things will no longer be the way they used to be. (*Upon that statement, God, angrily wakes up from his seat and goes around, speechless. One of his archangels (Ndoki Machine) follows him.*)

ACT 1: SCENE 2

[God has felt offended by Satan's statement. Consequently he walked away in the hall passage, leaving him alone seated for a while)

Ndoki Machine (Coming *from behind and inviting God aside)*

May I intervene, my Lord?

God (*He does not turn back nor answer. Satan comes from behind and passes by*)

Ndoki Machine

My Lord.

God

Yes, Machine.

Ndoki Machine

May I insert a word in your talk, Your Majesty? (*God lets Satan continue the round and leans his ears to the side of the speaking Ndoki Machine.*) This man, as you warned us earlier, seems to be untenable.

God

He knows more. Therefore he should be watched. There is no dreaming about his presence here. Otherwise, we'll be taken aback by his deceitful tactics. He knows more, Satan. Yes, he does.

Ndoki Machine

"More?" What does he know after such a long absence from you and after various reshuffles of this celestial cabinet?

God (*After a long gaze.*)

He is privy to everything.

Ndoki Machine

"To everything?" Say it again my Lord! What everything?

God

The secret of creation. Your creation. Me, and just everything. He knows. This is my mistake. I trusted him too much. (*Showing signs of regret.*)

Ndoki Machine

What? Do you mean this guy . . . ?

God.

You, as a lawyer, should imagine a formula to find a common ground of understanding between us. Sorry. I meant to say, between me and Mr. Satan. Allow me to warn you that, in this upper State of universe we are living in, you should not take this case lightly. It goes with the survival of all of us, or . . .

Ndoki Machine

Or what, my Lord? This man deserves nothing more than banishment from either planet. As long as he does not appreciate the multiple advantages you had offered him, he . . .

God

Hey! There you come now. Of course, favours that he can't find anywhere else. Those advantages are unique.

Ndoki Machine

You see. He deserves nothing other than final degradation and confinement to a more isolate abode, where he wouldn't be in touch with anybody else, because he is just a public menace. A *pariah*.

God

Wait a minute. (*Grabbing his hand.*) Is it the legal formula you've thought of?

Ndoki Machine

Not yet, but, *per se*, it may be a solace for you as well as for the whole universe should you get rid of this nagging guy. He seems to be treating you as a gofer. How dares he speak to you in an unceremonious manner like that, yet he well knows that you are his creator? You are God; the supreme one.

God

Wait, Machine. Please, wait. (*The Chief Protocol arrives to interrupt.*)

Chief Protocol.

My Lord, Mr. Satan is exhibiting some signs of impatience, I mean, one can read aggressiveness on his forehead; that means he is craving to continue speaking to you, as the talk was not finished yet.

Ndoki Machine

Chief, you'd rather tell him to return where he comes from instead of pressuring people here. We are in a consultation corner here, and there is no reason for a rush.

Chief Protocol

Okay, okay, okay.

Ndoki Machine Tell him to subdue himself to the protocol tenets. Otherwise, we will confiscate his diplomatic passport, and he may be sued for a *lèse-majesté* count and be jailed here. We don't joke here.

God (*To Ndoki Machine.*)

Take it easy, Machine. That man is dangerous and unpredictable. We should be tactful and tactical with him. Otherwise, he may desecrate everything here.

Chief Protocol

You mean? Your majeste?

God

That guy may cause mayhem here. He is . . . he is just an angry type, a power-hungry character who will never be satisfied no matter how much share you offer him.

Chief Protocol. My Lord!

God

Go tell him that I am coming. In the meantime, show him the beautiful paintings and artistic landscape around the hall.

Chief Protocol (*Bowing.*)

I am much obliged, Your Highness.

God (*Turning to Ndoki Machine.*)

You zip your mouth as we reach there. Understand?

Ndoki Machine

Yes, I do.

God

Whatever excrement he will release, I will mop it up wisely so that the final victory is ours. Understand?

Ndoki Machine

Your Majesty. (*Bowing.*)

God

You should understand that, no man can vanquish Mr. Satan. He is my sole creation masterpiece that I have made. And only I can reverse the process, should this monstrous and rebellious automaton get angry one day.

Ndoki Machine (*stares at him and does not say anything; then he nods.*)

God

Delay your following me. Let me meet him alone while you members remain still just over there. (*Ndoki Machine just looks at him silently. Then God walks in the majestic hall alone while cabinet members rise and bow in silence. In his imperial attire, God gets seated, facing Satan.*)

ACT 1: SCENE 3

Satan

Your anger took long to dissipate, sir.

God

Well. What can I do? Of course, it should. Anger melts like a lit candle. One should not rush it.

Satan

You never change. Ever since you were hijacked by your adviser, you become inexorable, always expecting people to pamper you, to kneel in front of you, to beseech you and sing your thanks and praises, even though you are wrong and failing to materialize the illusionary promises that you made unto men and all of us. You're too babyish with all this!

God

You, too, never change. You remain that fault-finding boy I saw growing up in this yard, until I initiated you to all my mystics and taught you all the creation crafts. But all that seems not to quench your thirst of your own pride and glory aiming at limitless supremacy. Who do you think you are?

Satan

You would be suffering from amnesia in asking me such a misplaced question, comrade. Who am I? (*Then, he smiles.*) Are you kidding?

God. Yes. Who are you?

Satan (*Looks straight into God's eyes.*)

I am you, and you are me. We are one. Have you forgotten? In Genesis 1:26, in the idiot book to idiots, a book which decorates every stupid family house on Earth, you state, and I am quoting, "*Let us make man in our image.*"

God

So what?

Satan

Certainly, we did make man in our image. Come on comrade. You were not alone. But how come today you grab the shares of ownership of creation alone and label me as your creature? Do you say this to please your entourage?

God

Indeed, I did create you. And there is no debate on that.

Satan (*Laughs longingly.*)

Look, there is one thing that people ought to know about between you and me: that, our common story is like an egg and a hen. No one knows who preceded whom. Is it the hen that gave birth to the egg or the egg that gave birth to the hen and the coq? Just tell me. Perhaps I am drunk.

Ndoki Machine (*From afar.*)

Effectively, you look like one.

God

I had ordered you to shut up, but record the talk. This man is . . .

Ndoki Machine

My Lord, such a creature cannot be given a chance to torment every planet. It's time we put an end to his reign. Otherwise, a planetarian cataclysm of irrationality will engulf all of us.

Satan (*Turning towards Ndoki Machine.*)

Who are you? (*Standing up and going close to him, lifting Machine's chin.*) Since when do lackeys like you hijack the floor when big minds are conversing? (*Ndoki Machine removes Satan's hand from his chin.*)

Ndoki Machine

Leave me alone. Intruder.

Satan (*Frightening*)

I asked to know who you were. Piece of shit. I can incinerate you right away if you continue poking your stinky nose into this matter.

God

Sorry, comrade. Please, return to me. (*Satan retreats a bit.*)

Ndoki Machine (*Trembling with fear*)

I am Ndoki Machine, His Majesty's attorney, private and legal adviser. Are you satisfied now?

Satan (*Returning again.*)

You should stop your baseless academic interference in this talk. (*Then, on his way back to his seat.*) I am sorry if your lord forgot to tell you who I was. If he did, let me warn you that should you continue to poke your ugly nose in this matter, your minutes of existence are numbered. Better know me when alive than when you'll be dead. (*Seated.*)

God

Pardon me for the inconvenience, comrade. It's just an academic bulimia, nothing more. You know, learned people are like waterfalls. Without noise, the rivers run dry. Consequently, they must make some noise to stamp their presence on the ground.

Satan.

You must discipline your new collaborators. I, with my group that you call rebellious, we were not like these noisy empty cans you accommodate here. They make a lot of noise; too much noise that irritates cool minds like mine.

God

Once more, accept my apology, comrade Satan.

Satan

Well, comrade, we should end this talk before noon, for I have to look after my babies down there on Earth. Be informed that the world down there is in an immense turmoil as a group called the *Illuminati* wants to create a single world government to enslave the rest of the humanity.

God

What?

Satan

Yes, comrade. I think I should intervene and crush them before they overshadow me.

God

This is strange!

Satan

Yes, indeed. Hence, before noon, my delegation and I may return home to start attending to that issue.

Ndoki Machine

(P*uzzled, he looks in all directions.)* We have no seasons here, sir. We have no time line, no calendar, and no human needs. We don't die. We already have told you that.

Satan (*Turns around and looks at Ndoki Machine.*)

Still you? You don't want to stop? I am as well your master, and can reverse the energy that animates you and pushes you to disrespect me. I am God as well, my child. Yes, I am one too. Didn't he tell you? (*All the cabinet members are shaken. They all look towards God, who fails to say something.*)

Members

Bbbbbbu, but, bbbbut, Lord.

God (*Silences them with a finger sign on his lips.*)

Satan

Tell your beggars and gofers to vacate the hall before the worst occurs. I don't accommodate impoliteness.

God (*With a hand gesture, he orders them to vacate the hall.*)

ACT 2: SCENE 1

(The scene occurs still in the same hall, but with a different scenery decoration.)

Satan

You've done well, Your Majesty.

God

I hope now we can calmly talk and iron out all our frictions. Nonetheless, I abhor your reminding of past events between you and me in public. The past belongs to the past. You shouldn't exhume what was buried long ago. Otherwise, minds and bodies will boil up.

Satan

Of course I shouldn't, but at this grand juncture, there is a need to.

God

But my celestial cabinet members are not concerned about that. Consequently, it is irrelevant to evoke the past to them.

Satan

Given that; they need to know the background to our conflict. Otherwise, they'll end up being duped by you and will remain blindly loyal for no apparent reason.

God

Please, comrade, don't seed another rebellion again. I have reigned peacefully over them here since you left. I am no longer young as you left me. Consequently, I am not prepared to face a second rebellion in this abode. I may remain alone here without a servant, you see? And you well know how much I like being pampered, feared, and mostly praised.

Satan

If you don't satisfy my demands, you are inviting yet one more rebellion. Nonetheless, understand that my intention and my objective in coming here is not to raise people against you.

God

Thanks and praises to you, comrade. Really, I like that statement. It brings in more assurance.

Satan *(After staring at him)*

You have brainwashed people to believe that I am bloodthirsty, and yet you, yourself, demand blood in whatever sacrifice your followers should make.

God

Oh! Please don't say that again. There are points that are taboos, which you should not raise in public. Hey! Those are the nitty-gritty of our friendship. Remember.

Satan

Given that, but evil is always worthy of being exposed.

God

No people can enjoy happiness without bloodshed.

Satan

But you remain bloodthirsty, and this is manifested by the way you handled the evacuation of your so-called chosen people from Egypt. You killed all first-born males and ordered the smearing of blood on your so-called children's doorposts.

God

Oh! You are hurting me. Please, stop that.

Satan

As if this was not enough, you instructed them to kill all their way along until they abducted the land of Canaan.

God

That's enough for now. You are churning a blade in body.

Satan

Even those who rebelled against Moses when he brought the table of the Ten Commandments down from meeting with his god; you killed them all, a painful death. Yeah, you did.

God

Please, stop it, comrade.

Satan

So, between you and me, who really is bloodthirsty?

God (*Keeps quiet for a long time and then . . .*)

That was my people, you said?

Satan

Meaning?

God

Listen, on one side, I am a universal God, while on the other, when I care for a particular people, I become a local god. So, what happened to the Israelis was a private affair and has nothing to do with you other people.

Satan

Waoh! It sounds clear. So, you mean to say, there is a small god of Israel and a universal grand God?

God

Effectively.

Satan. Which one am I talking to now?

God

The one you've known ever since creation, but with one side shadowed.

Satan

Terrible.

God

There is nothing terrible in that, comrade. I am the God you know—since Eden, in the past; when you morphed into a reptilian to help charm Eve. I am the one now; and I will still be the same. You remember the fight between you and Archangel Michael in heaven. But do not think of the past events again. That is passed and should no longer haunt your memory.

Satan

It's just flabbergasting how you keep on referring to the past! Aren't you the one who was saying you don't have season or calendar in heaven?

God

Yes. It's us. Bbbbbut . . .

Satan

So, no event should be considered bygone. It's cyclical if not static; and there is no way we can settle this dispute without reviving the past comrade.

God

I am trying to understand. But, suffer that I discourage you from digging into the past. The past always stinks, you know.

Satan *(Pause)*

It seems you hold a great plan for the world, a marvellous plan. Which one, if I may ask?

God *(Having been absent-minded and jiggling a bit.)*

Pardon me. You were saying?

Satan

Is it not you who permitted me to carry forward my work on Earth?

God

Yes, of course I am the one. But I never asked you to carry it on to the level of revolting against me.

Satan

Since I went down onto the Earth, I orchestrated no rebellion against you. I have been carrying out my duties as per prescription, contractually and mutually.

God

Yes. So far so good; and congratulations.

Satan

Thanks. And yet, I am flabbergasted today to view and hear that I have been perverting humanity; that sin has entered the world through and by me, to the point that you raise an army of preachers who have nothing better to do than insult me, vilify me, accuse me of all sorts of evils that may exist in their world, and even put me on trial. How come you allow such a thing to happen, comrade?

God (*A bit cheerful.*) Look, look, look, Satan, calm down. Be quiet, comrade.

Satan

I am trying to.

God

Humanity is free, and I don't interfere with their justice system.

Satan

But who tells them that I am the Prince of Evil? Not you?

God

They make their own investigation. That's what I think.

Satan

Ah, no. You seem to be throwing a bone to a dog and holding a cane in your hand. Who created evil. Isn't it you?

God

Certainly, it's me. But, we agreed that you should play a counterpart role so we could select a better human being, who could assist us in all what we do. And . . .

Satan

True. But, where does all this horde of preachers come from? Them who keep on accusing me of corrupting the humanity and so forth and so on? I was humiliated on Earth once in my life, you know.

God *(Standing up and going towards Satan.)*

When was that? Who the hell tried that on you?

Satan

Be sincere with me. I am not content at all, because I was arrested and put on trial by frail creatures in a human court. I, being judged for doing the work you assigned me to do. How abnormal is that!

God

Sorry. Sorry. I can imagine the kind of humiliation you suffered; my friend. Yes, I can feel it.

Satan

You think I am nutty?

God

No. I don't. I really don't think so. I am just trying to figure out what could have been the reason for our creatures to harass you in that manner. Yet, they owe you full respect.

Satan

They claim they have a divine right, mixed up with human rights—something they call democracy or *demon crazy*; a strange ideology which you injected in their irrational minds and which is boosting their energy to act the way they please, disrespecting even a supreme master mind, which I am.

God

Pardon them, for they don't know who you are.

Satan

When will they know who I am? Are you fearful to divulge this crucial piece of information to them?

God

There's no need to publicize that you are my representative on Earth. Everybody is aware of that, ever since creation.

Satan (*After a long stare at him.*)

But we can't be two representatives on Earth? How many times do I have to remind you this?

God

You mean?

Satan

There is one guy on planet Earth who calls himself the Pope.

God

Gosh! Yes, go on.

Satan

Well, the guy's got plenty of appellations.

God

Like?

Satan

He calls himself, or rather they call him, "*The Pope, the pontiff, the holy father,* etc." This guy is a superstar on Earth, you see. He claims to be your sole representative there. And he has a huge following who blindly believe in him. Together, they celebrate masses, during which they insult me, accuse me of all the world's evils, and condemn me as the originator of their sufferings. How possible?

God (*A bit surprised.*)

Gosh! Save you, I never appointed anyone else to represent me on Earth. Never. I am afraid that what the Pope does against you is a usurpation of mandate. Who is this guy you call what? Popo, Pipi or Pappy? (*Satan smiles.*) Hey! Who is that man?

Satan

The Pope.

God

Oh yeah! That one. The pimp . . .

Satan (*Smiling.*)

It's a rich guy. He has assets everywhere in the world.

God

Does he account for them?

Satan

You mean?

God

I mean, him and his organization, do they pay taxes?

Satan

He claims he works for you, and that a church is NPO. Consequently, prior to its inception every church, synagogue, mosque, etc . . . has been exonerated of all its charges.

God

You mean?

Satan

A non-profit organization.

God (*Laughing.*)

He should be brought to books and clear all the arrears his organization owes to the world in order to alleviate poverty.

Satan

Not only him, but even you, too, are sought by the Earth's inhabitants for the many and false promises you've been giving them.

God (*Keeps quiet for a while, and then stares at Satan.*)

Start first with your neighbour, the Pope, and then I will follow suit. To ameliorate your living standard, you actually need the money that he has been stashing in his chests across the world. Only after that shall we see whether he still will be called "*Father of all nations*" or not.

Satan

How can he call himself "*the Father of all nations*"?

God

I think it's with your approval. You've got the power, but you do not use it. All that wouldn't have happened without your resignation.

Satan

My what? You really are enigmatic and self-destructive. I can't believe that you officially appoint me to rule the Earth on the one hand, while on the other you plant spies and challengers to sabotage my job description and my mission!

God

No, no, no, no, no.

Satan

How do you want me to work perfectly and deliver good services to you when you surround me with barbed wires and spikes all over the ground where I tread?

God

No, no, no, no. You're taking it further, comrade.

Satan

Every day and everywhere, I am being stalked by your army of crooks and charlatans, who arm themselves with a couple of "*holy books*" to seduce and sedate human minds in your name but end up amassing incommensurable wealth, for which they don't account. Gosh! These guys do not pay tax!

God

Oooooh, look at that. Ooooooh! So sad. Please, stop that train of unhappiness now.

Satan

Ravages are caused on planet Earth because of your silence and truancy on the terrain. Your army of seducers and liars feels free to do what pleases them because you keep quiet; consequently condoning evil practices, deceit and exploitation of the naïve; look now how much deceit is all over my jurisdiction.

God

I know that; it is taking time for me to intervene and denounce the wrong deeds the so-called "*servants of God*" are perpetrating on my beloved creatures. But also, on the one side, you failed to crush them, because I gave you the power to act like me, because you are me.

Satan *(After starring at him)*

I like the last part of your statement, comrade. But how long will these poor creatures called men still have to wait to see you making justice and removing the power of deceit from the hand of your army of pretenders, whose sole commercial product they sell is lie, lie, and lie?

God

Very soon. Very soon, comrade Satan. Just wait and see.

Satan

Very soon? But, "*very soon*" was the promise you gave them when you told them that your "*kingdom was coming.*" Very soon, and till today, that promised kingdom has never come! How pretty serious must the world believe in you when the first promises have never materialized?

God

God is God, and nobody is God. Thus, nobody can judge him. Not even you. He is sovereign, and the final word is his.

Satan

If such is the case, I therefore refuse to carry the burden of sins that I did not initiate. You gave firm promises of good life to human beings; you claim to have sent your so-called son, Jesus Christ, to die and wash away their sins so that they could enjoy a good living, but none of those promises has materialized! And I remain the lamb to be sacrificed for a wrong that I did not do? Which I never did besides.

God

Satan . . .

Satan

Yes, comrade.

God

There is a time when the truth will come out, and the pretenders will all be hurled into a furnace to burn, just like the drowning punishment suffered by those pigs that my son, Jesus Christ threw into that lake. I know that no man will claim he represents me on Earth when I open the gates of the heavens. None.

Satan

People are suffering because you are deserting from your responsibilities, and I have become your scapegoat to shield your failure. Given my loyalty to you and the respect of my job description, how long will I continue to play this perilous game of hypocrisy?

God

No.

Satan

In lieu of me being apprehended and humiliated as I once was and maybe still will be, you really are the person suited for a trial for failing to supply human beings with an abundant life as you promised.

God

Sorry.

Satan

Aren't you ashamed to lie to the humanity, but keep on requiring it to kneel down and chant praises and thanks to your glory?

God

Pathetic.

Satan

Why did you create man, first of all? Why did you park him on a planet of attritions, and condition him to worship you?

God

Don't take it far, comrade Satan. I see my Chief Protocol is beaconing there. I believe he's something to whisper to me. Mr. Satan, let's put off this important and friendly talk for another session. For, for the moment, you can enjoy the pleasure of our planet, and the Chief Protocol will always tell me when it will be suitable to resume this talk. Your security is ensured; our bodyguards are here for that; but I warn, don't indulge in any talk with them.

Satan

Why not?

God

They don't talk your language. Come. (*Calling Chief Protocol.*)

Satan

Still, you are an unreliable partner.

God

Stop it there. We will talk it over later.

(Both God and Satan leave the hall.)

ACT 2: SCENE 2

(God and Satan are seated face to face. *Some cabinet members of the Theocratical Republic of Heaven make their entrance in the hall and get seated.*)

Sperm Matozoid (*Comes and bows in front of God and plants a royal mast next to him.*) Long live His Highness.

Voltaire

What is that?

Sperm Matozoid

His Majesty God, the Most High, is symbolized in it, this mast. It is the token of energy and, at the same time, is an expression of his *grandeur* for having created the universe: heavens, earth, animals, waters, and, more especially, man; who is his masterpiece.

Voltaire (A *bit upset.*)

What? No, no, no, no. Masterpiece?

Sperm Matozoid

Any problem, sir?

Voltaire

Listen. We have come over here, to settle a dispute between His Excellency President Satan, and your creator, but not to praise him.

Sperm Matozoid

I concur with you, sir *(Exit.)*

Karl Marx

Hm! Go ahead.

Voltaire

Our president is hurt ever since he was appointed and sent to rule over our republic.

Mr. Kraft Buganga

In which way, sir?

Voltaire

Continue to sit down and strap in.

Mrs. Nda Kulya

We're listening to you, sir.

Voltaire

And I am not alone in this juncture. My colleague Mr. Karl Marx has a book presumably written or else dictated by your president.

Mr. Kasebo Lwenzo

And then . . .

Voltaire

How does your president claim to have created us alone, yet this book you make us call "*holy*" says the contrary of his pretentions?

Kasebo Lwenzo

Eh eh! You must pay attention to what you say, sir. His Most High does not pretend. He is what he says, and he has said. So, as human beings that you are, you'd better watch out.

Voltaire

We are used to intimidations, bullying, and blackmailing tactics on Earth, sir.

Karl Marx

Yes, Voltaire; tell him. Every day, we are accused of having killed Jesus Christ and are told that our ancestors sinned and that sins became endemic and started mutating one generation from another.

Voltaire

Would you please pass me that book called *Bubble Gum*—oh, sorry, the Christian Bible gun?

(*Enter both God and Satan; everybody rises. Then they get seated.*)

Karl Marx (*Pulling it out of a leather attaché case and handing it to Voltaire.*)

Here you are.

Voltaire

Thanks, my man.

Karl Marx

Pleasure.

Voltaire

Your Majesty (*Addressing God.*), I am still appalled by the statement of your ministers and the silence that followed after one of them, . . . eh; this Mr. Sperm Matozoid has again wounded us in confirming that you are the creator of the universe and, more particularly, of us human beings.

God

There is no doubt about that. I made you, and I can unmake you anytime I want.

Voltaire

Bbbbbut . . . . how come?

(*Sperm Matozoid stands up and sounds irate*)

Sperm Matozoid

Don't ever ask that question again. The era of rebellion against God has long gone. His Majesty can no longer tolerate or allow such a disruptive attitude from ungrateful persons like you.

Voltaire

What!

Ndoki Machine

If you are a philosophical trade unionist, it is time you pack up your stuff and return where you came from. This is a republic of tranquility, wherein no new idea shakes the established institutions.

Voltaire *(Flipping through pages in the Bible.)*

Don't quote me wrong, sirs. I am not disrupting anything here. It is our right to know what the allegations of your president's *status quo* are . . .

Ndoki Machine

There is no question of *status quo*. Do you understand? God is; he has been and will always be. You, you are trying the impossible.

Voltaire

Yet, in this book the truth is otherwise.

Mrs. Nda Kulya

This is the word of God. You can't challenge it.

Voltaire

We reject mind manipulation as well as programming. Look; in these two passages from the book of Genesis; the plurality of gods who decided to create a human survives and resists the test of the lying time.

God (A *bit shaken from his seat.*)

What!

Voltaire

You were not alone, sir, when you allegedly created us. Isn't it so?

Chief Protocol

Blasphemy, blasphemy. Your Majesty, banish him so that he lives no more. Please, banish this insubordinate creature.

Voltaire

This is madness!

Ndoki Machine

You dare talk like that to His Majesty?

Voltaire (*who remains unshaken.*)

Genesis 1:26-27 says: "*And God said, Let us make man in **our** image, after **our** likeness. So God created man in his own image, in the image of God created he him, male and female created he them.*"

Chief Protocol

Listen to that.

Karl Marx (*To that, God and his cabinet members look around.*)

Still, in the same book, 3:22 is said what follows: "*And the Lord God said, Behold, the man is become as one of **us,** to know good and evil, and now, lest he put forth his hand, and take also of the tree of life, and eat, and live forever.*"

Chief protocol

Listen to that.

Voltaire

Sir, from that viewpoint, it is proven that you were not alone when you created the universe, more especially us, your supposedly stupid human beings. Surely, you were with someone!

God

Someone?

Voltaire

Certainly, you were with someone else, in addition to yourself. Someone or, allow me to say, *someones*. A full team of creators. It is therefore astonishing to see how you and your propagandists on Earth try to impose the opinion on us that you are the sole creator. No. You are a cheat, sir.

Ndoki Machine

I warn you, sir. I am the minister of Justice in this republic. And should you not adhere to the principles of negotiation and conflict resolution, I will have no other alternative than to expel you from the panel and walk you out of this majestic hall.

God's cabinet members

Good. Very good.

Joseph Stalin

You have no right whatsoever to do that, sir. We haven't wasted our time to come and reach you over here just to be chased away like beggars, for asking to know the truth. This is our democratic right.

Ndoki Machine

Please, keep quiet.

Karl Marx

If you are minister of Justice in this republic, it therefore means that a lot of injustices are being committed here. Which contradicts what one of your colleagues said a while ago, that you "enjoy tranquility" in here.

Kasebo Lwenzo

Tranquility is no synonymous of absence of problems. Listen; we are hosting you here. You have no liberty to judge us. And there is nothing that you people can teach us.

Joseph Stalin

It is because of your lies that I created communism in the Soviet Union, a doctrine under which my regime legally massacred many so-called Christians who behaved like you. It was a self-defense mechanism against religious onslaught on us. You sound dictatorial and are not prepared to listen to somebody else's opinion.

God

My people are doing their job, Mr. Stalin.

Satan

Mine too, comrade. The fact is, your misrule has imposed and has been promoting a prevalence of much lies in our republic. It's an anomaly.

God

How?

Satan

My team told you. Your priests, pastors, Popes, brothers and sisters in Christ, your churches and mosques, all those sanctuaries of mind programming have devastated our republic. And you don't want my people to demand an explanation from you? This is tyrannical! Undemocratic. Down there, my people are not used to the inanity of opinion like here. They talk, they challenge my utterances. Reason why they once put me on trial.

Go

I am eternal. Therefore everything relating to me must prevail everywhere. None can set boundary where my work is to be implemented.

Satan (*A bit angered.*)

My people can no longer accommodate the implantation of these multinationals of lies in their midst. So, you and your cabinet members owe them clear cut explanation;

and mostly, you have to guarantee them when will you stop this trend of churches, mosques and synagogues everywhere in our republic.

God

This should be done in politeness. And remember, I am God.

Jean-Paul Sartre

Meaning?

God

Greedy on deeds. Do you understand? Greedy on deeds. That means I don't share my decisions with someone else. I don't consult anybody else; I dismiss everyone's opinion. I am not accountable to anyone, and I am irreproachable.

Jean-Paul Sartre

But all this is terrible. How dare you talk like that, Your Majesty?

God

You people seem to have forgotten the agenda that brought you in here. If you experience shortages of assets in your poor republic, just say it. Don't beat around the bush. You sound bitter and antogonistical.

Jean-Paul Sartre

Your Majesty. Let us talk about the curse of Cain, who according to Christianity, Islam, and Judaism, is said to have been Adam's firstborn.

God

Yes, we are listening.

Jean-Paul Sartre

Thanks. In the book of Genesis, Cain is described as "*the wicked one*" allegedly after killing his brother Abel. Then you cast him away. Then he got a wife, with whom he got a child. Is that right?

God

That's right.

Jean-Paul Sartre

Tell us, Your Majesty; where did he get his wife, yet after the alleged death of his brother only three creatures were living on Earth at that time?

Kasebo Lwenzo

His Most High is not obliged to answer such a silly question.

Jean-Paul Sartre

What! Silly question?

Kasebo Lwenzo

Really silly. You must . . .

God (*Intervening abruptly.*)

Please, stop it. Let me answer it. You see Sartre, in that era; the Earth was not as populated as it is nowadays. The couple Adam and Eve did not know that I hid other people in a neighboring land; those who had to replace them in an event of their mischievousness. It is where Cain got his spouse.

Jean-Paul Sartre

Were those people worshipping you as well like us? Were there religious cults and preachers like in our era?

God

At that time, human beings had not started sinning yet. Faith and worship stemmed from the weakness of man's disobedience. And, as man had no other means to approach me, he created religious channel to communicate with me; but; frankly speaking, I never asked human being to worship me. In any case, as long as praises and worships make me grand, they are welcome. It's all fine with me.

Kasebo Lwenzo

You see. You must praise the Most High.

Satan

It's not what he's saying. Why are you extrapolating? Yourselves up here; why don't you have a multitude of churches and mosques here?

Joseph Stalin

In addition, why don't you have pastors, preachers, the so-called brothers and sisters in Christ and Popes up here? The Earth is awash with many cult movements, which have established an insane environment that has a brainwashing effect on the unwary. Some bizarre religions do the unthinkable . . .

Kasebo Lwenzo

Nobody pushes you to go there. Please, stop assailing His Majesty with those futile questions about religions. This is not an interrogation room; you know.

Jean-Paul Sartre

It's strange! But why? It's apparent that you are not happy at all when we scratch the wall of your citadel of mind manipulation and crooking practices!

Kasebo Lwenzo

You created religions on Earth; not us up here; not even God. It's your scheme. Now, as you notice the widening schism, you're looking for a scapegoat. His Majesty did say it. What more do you want?

God (*Talking to Kasebo.*)

Take it easy, Kas . . . easy. We are not fighting here.

(*Satan Smiles*)

Joseph Stalin

But Your Majesty, religion on Earth is to be looked at as an industry. We have records from our planet proving new products are being dished out in recent times. The Jehovah's Witnesses, The Way, Mormons, the Moonies, Children of God, Scientology, Rajneesh, and many corner shop churches created by some miserable and cunning

Africans that are ripping off the lonely and naïve minds, some spiritually disaffected, who expect to get solace in a jungle of suckers.

God

That is extrapolation, Mr. Joseph. Democratically speaking, it is a theocratic right to worship one's creator. There is nothing wrong in that!

Joseph Stalin

There, Your Majesty. The cunning ones are piteously and spiritually robbing the gullible ones, who are not rationally armed; more particularly, the poor and the spiritually immature Africans.

Karl Marx

True. Most of these religious cults have large followings worldwide. They have started many offshoot branches at each street corner; but nothing tangible comes out there except intimidation, calumny, and conditioning of the weakest and the naïve ones.

God's cabinet members

Hmmmmmmmm! He is raving.

Voltaire

What we know is that former as well as current members of these religious syndicates are victims of subtle brainwashing techniques to ensure absolute obedience to the leaders of these sects, who plunge them into an illusion of welfare, painless living or else eternal life. People are poor and afraid to suffer and die, you know.

God's cabinet members

Hmmmmmm! Ohhhhhhh!

Voltaire

Followers of these syndicates are sheepish and cannot question any order or statement at all from their super tricksters and professional crooks who label themselves prophets, seers, miracle-operators and who are nothing but a group of vicious impellers.

God's cabinet members

No, no, no, no, no, no. Stop that calumny. Stop it.

Jean-Paul Sartre

The ugliest part of it all is, once one is initiated to religious intimidation rules and rites, one begins to be enmeshed in the obscure rules, which are cleverly designed to enslave them and keep them in perpetual bondage. Total submission.

God's cabinet members

Stop it. Enough jokes now. Stop.

Voltaire

Yet, your son kept on telling us he was the way, the truth, and the light. Where is that grandiose promise when people are being *shepherded* like cattle?

God (*Standing up from his seat.*)

Wait, wait, you ignorant creatures. When Jesus said, "*I am the way, the truth, and the light,*" for example, he was really referring to everyone's "I," which means that part of me, me the Absolute, which is present in every one of you. The same Jesus said, "*The kingdom of God is within you*". And out of that, you must discover yourself and stop being misled by false prophets. Come on, men. Even your government should protect you against conmen. Why did it abandon you?

Satan

Hang on a second, my friend (T*o God*). Let me tell you this story.

God

Yes, go on.

Satan

Pleasure. While attending a public Mass at Saint Peter's palace in Rome, I circumvented the place and while hovering above the roof atop which the Pope was giving his speech, I was baffled by some inscriptions on the Pope's mitre.

God

I'd be pleased to be informed by you. Go ahead.

Satan

The letters inscribed on the Pope's mitre are these: "*Vicarius Filii Dei,*" which is Latin for "Vicar of the Son of God," spiced with the mystic figure 666. Behold.

Ndoki Machine

His Majesty has never appointed that guy as his representative on Earth. We already have told you that.

Satan

No, no, no, no, no, no. Get me well, sir. I said, "Vicar of the son of God." It has nothing to do with your previous statement.

Ndoki Machine

Which means? I mean, go on.

Satan

A vicar is a person who substitutes in the office of a principal person when that person is not present. Consequently, a vicar has all the authority of the principal person during the principal's absence. And in this case . . .

Lunyego Kitwanda

As minister of Defense, I will not allow you to continue assailing His Majesty with such a barrage of useless questions and baseless litany of your *reverie*.

Karl Marx

Useless? What is useless in what the president is questioning?

Lunyego Kitwanda.

Yes, useless. Your president is supposed to know the meaning of all he seeks to know, because he is the one who rules over the Earth. His Majesty God delegated him onto your planet. Consequently, nothing can escape his intelligence. But, this is not an appropriate venue to ask such a question. You've been told this before.

Karl Marx

You've misled us, sir. Let me help you. My colleague needs to know why the Pope of the Roman Catholic Church is called a "*substitute of Jesus Christ on our Earth*." That's that. Why?

Lunyego Kitwanda

Ask him. Ask the Pope. He surely knows why he awarded himself with such a title. We don't entertain such libels here. And, His Majesty God cannot be answerable for that. Direct your trivial questions to Earth rulers, not us. His Majesty needs a rest.

Satan

My dear friend, (*Looking at God.*) I find it deceitful from you in this mutual division of work to have appointed me President of the Republic of Earth, yet, at the same time, two other guys represent you there.

God

Who are those?

Satan

Jesus Christ and the Pope of Rome. This is not serious.

God

One of them is my son: Jesus Christ. But the other guy, who calls himself Pope, is just an impostor. I don't know what else to tell you as you you refuse to be persuaded. I have never appointed him, and he does not know me. Neither do I entertain any communication flow with him. Again, he should know that I did not create any religion. Those who talk on my behalf are just money mongers who tarnish my holy name and hijack my authority whenever I am relaxing.

Joseph Stalin

Oh! So even you, you take time to relax also?

God

Why not? I work hard; that's why . . .

Joseph Stalin

May we still maintain that you are omnipresent?

God

I never said that. Never. But I accept whichever qualifications they paste on me as long as it elevates my power and glory; it's welcome for me.

Jean-Paul Sartre

Bbbbbut, let us go back to this guy called the Pope.

God

Yes, Mr. Jean-Paul Sartre. You seem to be interested in him.

Jean-Paul Sartre (*Smiles a bit.*) Look; I wrote many books about you and him. In some of those books, I tried to defend you, and in the others, the Pope wouldn't survive my attacks. He therefore excommunicated me, calling me names such as "*atheist, demoniac, pagan, anti-Christ,* etc." Simply because . . .

God

You did well in defending yourself. But, frankly speaking, the Pope and his army of priests, nuns, and other mythomaniacs are just a nag in me.

Satan

Are they? Okay. Let us revisit this word "*vicar.*" If the Pope can replace your alleged son, Jesus Christ, on Earth, that simply means your "son" died forever or left the world forever, and this guy who calls himself Pope is your second son by proxy process?

God

I never said that. You know, comrade, I think you are the one who fails to discipline this guy by allowing him to build a great empire of lies and striking deals with heads of states to open up offshoot branches of his wrangling network. Had it been me on Earth, he would already have seen fireworks.

Joseph Stalin

During my reign in my country, Russia, I closed down all his futile industry of lies, killing priests and other devouts and charlatans who were opposed to Communism and Socialism. With the help of my comrades, such as Trotsky, we culled the Christian population out there, because the membership was becoming a plague nationwide.

God

You did pretty well in reducing that overpopulation of mind jailers. People like you are good soldiers that I need here in heaven to guard all the borders between us and your morally polluted planet. Because; of late, suspicious reconnaissance movements of UFOs piloted by hungry Earth dwellers have been spotted around here.

Satan

You wouldn't do that.

God

I beg your pardon.

Satan

You wouldn't ex-filtrate one soldier among my subjects on Earth. I warn you, it may lead to an interplanetary confrontation between you and me.

God

Well, I didn't intend to . . .

Satan

Ah! No. Let it end there. Look, in John 16:7, your so-called son says this: "*Nevertheless I tell you the truth; it is expedient for you that I go away: for if I go not away, the Comforter will not come to you; but if I depart, I will send him to you.*"

Lunyego Kitwanda

Well, read John 14:26 to know who the Comforter is.

Jean-Paul Sartre

"But the Comforter, who is the Holy Ghost, whom the Father will send in my name, he shall teach you all things, and bring to your remembrance, whatsoever I have said unto you."

Lunyego Kitwanda

Now, you see. The Comforter is the Holy Ghost, who is often referred to as the Holy Spirit. He is the *vicar* of the son of God. Not the Pope.

Karl Marx

You mean the Pope lies? He is a sort of pretender?

Lunyego Kitwanda

Exactly. Something like that.

Jean Paul Sartre

Who then, between him and the ordinary man, *blasphemises* the most?

Lunyego Kitwanda

Never believe the lies of pretenders.

God

Indeed, do not. Sweet talkers are great deceivers.

Satan

But, comrade, there is an unfinished business here. (*To God.*) Finally, how many representatives will you have on Earth? I, Jesus, the Pope, and now this intruder called Holy Spirit. How can a ghost be holy? Someone who scares imagination and causes havoc in his passage. How?

God

Beloved comrade Satan; only my son, Jesus, was appointed to rule the Earth and represent me. But, after you and your people had rejected him and killed him, he ascended to come and live with me here. Consequently, nobody else could fit that position, save you. You my best friend, Satan. *(All his cabinet members are amazed, and suspiciously they look at one another.)*

Satan *(Raising his hands and smiling.)*

What an honor, gentlemen, what a memorable moment in my career!

Satan's delegation

Viva the President, viva. Viva His Excellency, Mr. President, viva. Viva, viva, viva *(All God's cabinet members are amazed, and then look at one another again.)*

God

Well *(Looking at his cabinet members.)*, it's clear.

God's cabinet members

Your Majesty, your Majesty; please do not barter your authority with the intrusion of these people. We can deport them from our planet as soon as possible if you permit it.

God

Ssssshhhhhh! Let us handle the case professionally, gentlemen.

God's cabinet members

But how? How?

God

Return to your seats. Mr. Satan is walking toward me. *(They all return to their seats.)*

Satan

My minister of Thought and Doubts, Mr. René Descartes, has a fundamental question for you, comrade God.

God

I am much obliged.

René Descartes

Your Majesty, there on Earth, the Catholic Church tells us that when we die we either go to heaven or go to purgatory or else to hell, if we are not saved. But mostly, we live haunted, from birth to death, by the fear of flames of fire that will burn us to ashes. Today, we have the unique chance to visit heaven. Therefore and kindly, can you take us on a round visit to see that purgatory and the hell too?

God *(Looks confused and seems not to understand.)*

Wwwwwwhat do you say?

René Descartes

Well, maybe I am the one who did not formulate well my request. Nonetheless, at least, as we are in heaven, can we visit the city of the holies, I mean those who died on Earth and whom, by your secret selection, joined you here?

God (*Laughing.*)

Such a thing as paradise does not exist; René. Even your president knows it; before he descends down there, that, there does not exist a city called Paradise here. All in all, it is a manipulator's scam.

René Descartes

You mean, saints, angels, and cherubim are not here?

God

You're free to search around and return to me with evidence of all those bollocks.

Mrs. Nda Kulya

On that point, dear Descartes, I should recommend you to read Ecclesiastes 9:5, 6, and 10. It will inform you about the fate of the deads.

René Descartes

I will read those passages; but learn that we live in an absolute fear on Earth. There is an urgent need to know . . .

Mrs. Nda Kulya

John 5:28-29 says this: *"Marvel not at this: for the hour is coming, in which all that are in the graves shall hear his voice, and shall come forth, they that have done good, unto the resurrection of life, and they that have done evil, unto the resurrection of damnation."*

René Descartes

You mean to say our fear is unjustifiable?

Mrs. Nda Kulya

Effectively. You can do wrong or good, pray or not pray; you'll end up dying, and all will rise up again. But we have no accommodation for walking bodies here. We are spirits. So never can we experience accommodation shortage.

Karl Marx

So regardless of whether they are saved or not, everyone will be resurrected from death? Is that what you mean?

Mrs. Nda Kulya

Exactly. Your body dies but not your spirit. It's just like a computer hardware that becomes obsolete, but the software continues to exist after you have gotten rid of the CPU box.

Karl Marx

Superb explanation. And, in addition to that, shall we say that these stories of Virgin Mary, who is still alive and being worshipped, are all hoaxes?

Mrs. Nda Kulya

They are. Yes, they are hoaxes. I can't say much on that fairy tale

Karl Marx

But what about the many people who have seen visions of the Virgin Mary and talked with her in their visions?

Mrs. Nda Kulya

On that note, I refer you to the holy book of 2 Corinthians 11:13-15. Don't be passionate about reveries narrated by some imbeciles.

Karl Marx (*Opens the Bible and silently reads the passage, which he finds offensive to their president, Mr. Satan*).

You therefore directly accuse our president of metamorphosing himself into Mary to tempt people?

Mrs. Nda Kulya (*Remains silent. Satan asks for the Bible, and in his turn silently reads the passage.*)

Satan (*Throws the Bible down.*)

You see, you see? (*Addressing God*) This is the reason that brought us here too. Still the same. Even your people here behave the same way as those I am supposed to rule over them on Earth.

God (*Standing up and holding Satan's hand.*)

Calm, calm, dear comrade. That was a glitch in my minister's speech. Also, you should not forget that not all that is in that book was dictated by me, dear friend. I told you, right from the start, that the writers of that book are flatterers and quite often blackmailers too. How could they have scribed abominable things like these? Yet, it is you and me who created the world, hey! Never was I consulted during the drafting of this.

Satan

I can't understand it.

God

They have perpetuated this row between us for their petty appetites. I strongly condemn that book because, truly speaking, it brings confusion. How can the book be called "holy" while there are a lot of atrocities and events of blood-shedding in it?

Satan

It's offensive and horrifying!

God

I know, but, believe you me; it won't be long before I send my son onto the Earth again to confuse all detractors, pretenders, blackmailers, and false prophets who claim to be my servants. You are my servant, not them.

Satan

No, no, no, no. I serve nobody's purpose! You forget? We drafted for each one of us a job description after we had split. I do what I ought to do, and that's that. I cannot be your servant anymore, for we are two worlds apart.

74

God

You sound too quick to decide, comrade.

Satan

Besides, I have never been your servant, but your accomplice, rather.

God

I am sorry, comrade. (*Each returns to his seat. With his fingers, God orders the woman (i.e., Nda Kulya) to leave the discussion hall.*)

ACT II: SCENE 3

God

Fine. We can proceed.

Joseph Stalin

In Titus 1:2, Your Majesty, you promised us human beings eternal life in these terms: *"In hope of eternal life, which God that cannot lie, promised before the world began."* However, we keep on dying every day! Isn't this a lie, Your Majesty?

Ndoki Machine

Eihn! Watch out, there is no way that His Majesty can lie. There can be no contradictions in what His Majesty has inspired. My friend, don't misinterpret that sanctified human book.

God (*To Stalin.*)

Did you get that?

Joseph Stalin

Funny. However, when I refer to a verse where Jesus said to the thief on the cross before he allegedly died on a Friday evening that they would meet that very day in paradise, a promise which failed to materialize, I find it, too, an instance of lie and contradiction in the Bible, sir.

Ndoki Machine

Which one?

Joseph Stalin (*To Descartes*).

Please, give me that book. In Luke 23:42-43, it is said, "*And he said unto Jesus, Lord, remember me when thou comest into thy kingdom. And Jesus said unto him, verily I say unto thee, today shalt thou be with me in paradise.*"

God's cabinet members

And then?

Joseph Stalin

How could Jesus have told the thief that he would be with him in paradise that day when Jesus himself had not gone to paradise yet? Because . . .

God's cabinet members

Bbbut, he . . .

René Descartes

Sunday morning, Jesus was seen talking with Mary and telling her that he had not yet been to paradise!

Joseph Stalin (Staring *at God and his cabinet members.)*

What do you say now, *eihn*! (All *God's cabinet members remain deeply silent.*)

Jean-Paul Sartre

Same lie and contradiction is found in John 20:16-17. It's just unbelievable!

God

Gentlemen, can we offer you some wine? We've been talking for such a long time.

Jean-Paul Sartre

Anything else, except that beverage.

God

Why? If I may ask.

Jean-Paul Sartre

Any beverage called wine transforms us human beings into cannibals or vampires.

God

What is that now, Sartre?

Jean-Paul Sartre

Isn't it your alleged son Jesus Christ who ordered that humans would be drinking his blood each time they have to take wine? This depicts that you people here are always bloodthirsty. You kill us to suck our blood in order to reinforce your energy; reason why on Earth we die in millions daily.

God

I don't think so. That was only on a unique occasion; he did that to his beloved disciples before his departure. And . . .

Jean-Paul Sartre

But he recommended that such a bloody ritual should continue. And here I quote. *"This is my body that I give unto you.*

This is my blood that I give unto you. Do this in the remembrance of me."

And that is found in Mathew 26:26, Luke 22:19, and Mark 14:22, etc.

Besides, where is he?

God

Who?

Jean-Paul Sartre

That guy called Jesus. Your so-called son.

God

After a long silence. Well, he was here a few minutes before your arrival.

Satan

And now?

God

If you thoroughly read the Bible in Mathew 28:20 (*"And surely I am with you always, to the very end of the age."*), Jesus himself would inform you that he never left the Earth. How could he, because in John 8:40, he tells you that he is just a human being like you. But you refuse and fail to understand and instead, you elevate him to a divine rank.

Stalin

But in John15:10, Jesus says the contrary!

God

We would love to hear that.

Stalin

Marx; would you please read John 8:40. (*"As it is, you are determined to kill me, a **man** who has told you the truth that I heard from God."*) All along, since this saga of Jesus started, I was right to disbelieve in it; reason why I butchered all these so-called Christians in the gulags.

God

The world will always remember you, Stalin.

Stalin

Thanks, Your Majesty.

Satan

Comrade God; my minister here (*Pointing at Stalin.*) is saying something of capital importance, which prompts me to ask a question. Who actually is the anti-Christ? Is it me, who challenges him, some of my human people who don't believe in him, or Jesus himself?

Ndoki Machine

Your Majesty, allow me to answer that question.

God

Please, go ahead, Machine.

Ndoki Machine

Look, the fact that you never recognized him as God-incarnate, and you bring yourself here with a delegation of *faith-gaugers,* proves that you are the one.

(Satan looks at his delegation members.)

Voltaire

But in the last passage read by Joseph Stalin, Jesus himself confirms that he is as human as we are. We should not miss that crucial affirmation of a Christ who is against himself.

Satan

That's perfect, Voltaire. But, comrade God; what do you call a man who proclaims himself "*the substitute of the son of God or else substitute of God himself.*"? Isn't that the one to be called anti-Christ?

Ndoki Machine

And who is it?

Satan

As I said earlier on, the Pope of Rome. He is the one. Yet, you keep on aiming all your guns at me.

God

Sorry, comrade Satan. Can I hit this issue off with you in private? Chief Protocol.

Chief Protocol

Your Majesty.

God

You, with all the members, please leave us alone for a while.

Chief Protocol

At your orders, Your Majesty. (*Bowing and beckoning all the cabinet members to follow him . . .*)

René Descartes

Before we all leave, your Majesty, can your Majesty allow me to pose a slight question?

God

It's allowed.

René Descartes

In Acts 17:25, you state that you *"give us life, breath, and everything."*

God

That's right.

René Descartes

Do you sometimes take time to cast your eye on Earth and realize in what turmoil we are living?

God

The problem with you, my creatures, is laziness. As your father, you are convinced that I will supply you with everything you like, at any time, by simply evoking my name. However, it isn't like that. And it shouldn't be like that at all.

Karl Marx

How? Apart from you, who else should spoil us with happiness and living abundance?

God

Material life, I mean the happiness most of you look for, is not stored in churches, mosques, or in any formula! Life is always ordered through natural mystic. It takes you to discover it and enjoy it.

Karl Marx

Is it?

God

Really, I am tired and often embarrassed with all the noisy prayers, enchanting songs, and somersaulting dances that you perform for me. All the preachings and speculations you spread over my name are invading my privacy. And, I repeat, take this message to the inhabitants of the planet Earth: things will change after this private encounter with your president.

René Descartes

Let us hope so.

God

No. Believe me. I never appointed anyone to speak on my behalf. Never.

Stalin

You see. (*Looking at his colleagues*)

God

Truly speaking, every one of you must find his spiritual identity and side to which he belongs; for I don't recall one day having met or spoken to a human being after his fall!

Voltaire

Is that true?

God

Cerainly. How, then, can some of you testify that I speak to them, that they meet me, and all the blah, blah, blah.

Voltaire

So strange.

God

The last time I met a human being was after I molded it out of clay. I retired after giving it a breath and the entire rational faculty. The last time a human being heard my voice was when I pronounced this sentence. "*By the sweat of your brow you will eat your food until you return to the ground, since from it you were taken, for dust you are and to dust you will return.*" Check it in Genesis 3:19.

And that was all. So, how can you speak about someone you have never met? Aren't human species mythomaniacs?

René Descartes

But, Your Majesty, once again, allow me to insist on this point that, the Earth is awash with armies of prophets, pastors, bishops, and many other 'holies" who torment us down there with the surety of your promises. They are your intermediaries. Why do you allow such prevalence of falsehood?

God

I said I don't know them. And, I need nobody to speak on my behalf.

(Satan laughs)

Chief Protocol *(Interrupting, and speaking to Satan's delegates.)* Okay. You of the Earth, please enter that room over there, while you here, of the Heaven, follow me toward this cenacle. His Majesty, God, wants to initiate a crucial and private parley with his guest, His Excellency, Mr. Satan, president of the Democratic Republic of Earth.

(*All sides leave separately. God and Satan are left face to face in the majestic hall.*)

ACT 3: SCENE 1

God

This one, comrade, I think, should be the meeting of the last chance to save the world from all sorts of calamities, allegations, accusations, blackmails, and gossips that have been spiking the drink of our relationship ever since we parted.

Satan

It's my solemn and absolute wish; for, I am lonely. Alone against your army of pretenders, who amass wealth, thanks to the lies they trade between you and me, taking advantage of our silence and truancy on a field that we almost left vacant, because of your fear and refusal to tell the truth to humanity; also, because of my hypocritical loyalty to you, I have been accepting all the accusations, swallowing all the trash and keeping quiet in order to protect you.

God

What else do you want me to do, comrade? The whole world knows pretty well that prior to creating Adam and Eve; you were the first magical creature I molded.

The world as well knows that I sent you to Earth to reign supreme. They know it. And if I cannot kill you or punish you, it is because . . . because . . . hey! Bbbbec.

Satan

Please finish, comrade. Because . . .

God

You and I, we created the man. They know it, even though they feign to not recognize it.

Satan

Will you one day take the courage to proclaim it u*rbi et orbi?* That means, publicly.

God

It is proclaimed in the Bible and other holy books!

Satan

You denied that; you are not the author or the inspirer of those trashes.

God

Kings sometimes condone many lies and flatteries, provided they concur with their grandeur and *imperium.*

Satan

And all that to my detriment?

God

It's regrettable, but there is nothing else that I can do against it. When the wine is served, one must drink it. It's regrettable that you remain an innocent scapegoat the humanity has been sacrificing.

Satan (*Starring at him; then pulls an attaché case out of his robe, laying it on the table.*)

Comrade, can you sign here, on this document, that you accept to step down from your seat and cede the power to me?

God (*A bit dubious.*)

Satan

If not, I will spill the beans to a greater proportion.

God

Don't do that; please don't. Remember, you are always welcome here any time you decide to visit. Give me a last chance to rectify any mistake I might have committed in the past.

Satan

Truly speaking comrade, you had had ample time to reverse the situation. All along it has been you, you and you only as the all saint, and me the villain.

God

We can settle this issue some other time; comrade.

Satan

Today's your last chance. You and your armies of "servants" and "witnesses" have been blackmailing me for crimes that I never committed. *(Raising his voice)* You cling onto power ever since I knew you; you dictate your single-handed laws; you promise happiness to the humanity but fail to honor your promises; and you tolerate dictatorship worldwide and keep the whole world in bondage. And the eternal culprit remains me. *(He takes a pause, then suddenly turns angry).* Sign this document. Sign it. Sign it now. *Bandit.*

(God is trembling and aiming at signing the resignation document when his cabinet members storm in to prevent him from signing. In this melee, one member of God's team makes the mistake of holding God's hand, but mistakenly forces it to sign the document. Satan snatches the document and keeps it in his mouth. Come in, all Satan's members, who witness to the battle. They join in, and a terrible combat occurs, which leaves all God's members utterly destroyed and God himself flies to an unknown place. Satan and his delegation proclaim victory on divine dictatorship, lie and incompetence. They board their space shuttle and return to Earth. Then they all sing along . . .)

Down, down, down with divine tyranny;

Down with the zero mighty God.

Down with God's bigotry

He must now be awash with infamy

Down, down, God is now drown *(Repeat and fade)*

Down, and released be the faith-jailed crowd.

No more cheating no more God's arrogance

Down o down with God's incompetence

Down, down, God is now drown *(Repeat and fade)*

End